EARLY BIRD
STORIES

Mine, Mine, Mine Said the Porcupine

Early ★ Reader

First American edition published in 2019 by Lerner Publishing Group, Inc.

An original concept by Alex English
Copyright © 2019 Alex English

Illustrated by Emma Levey

First published by Maverick Arts Publishing Limited

Maverick
arts publishing

Licensed Edition
Mine, Mine, Mine Said the Porcupine

For the avoidance of doubt, pursuant to Chapter 4 of the Copyright, Designs and Patents Act of 1988, the proprietor asserts the moral right of the Author to be identified as the author of the Work; and asserts the moral right of the Author to be identified as the illustrator of the Work.

Lerner Publications Company
A division of Lerner Publishing Group, Inc.
241 First Avenue North
Minneapolis, MN 55401 USA

For reading levels and more information, look up this title at www.lernerbooks.com.

Main body text set in Mikado a. Typeface provided by HVD Fonts.

Library of Congress Cataloging-in-Publication Data

Names: English, Alex, author. | Levey, Emma, illustrator.
Title: Mine, mine, mine said the porcupine / by Alex English ; illustrated by Emma Levey.
Description: First American edition, licensed edition. | Minneapolis, MN : Lerner
    Publishing Group, Inc., 2019. | Series: Early bird readers. Blue (Early bird stories).
Identifiers: LCCN 2018018055 (print) | LCCN 2018027519 (ebook) |
    ISBN 9781541543294 (eb pdf) | ISBN 9781541541733 (lb : alk. paper) |
    ISBN 9781541546158 (pb : alk. paper)
Subjects: LCSH: Readers—Play. | Readers—Friendship. | Readers—Sharing | Readers
    (Primary) | Play—Juvenile literature. | Friendship—Juvenile literature. | Sharing—
    Juvenile literature.
Classification: LCC PE1127.P56 (ebook) | LCC PE1127.P56 E54 2019 (print) |
    DDC 428.6/2—dc23

LC record available at https://lccn.loc.gov/2018018055

Manufactured in the United States of America
1-45347-38997-8/1/2018

EARLY BIRD
STORIES

Mine, Mine, Mine Said the Porcupine

Alex English

Illustrated by
Emma Levey

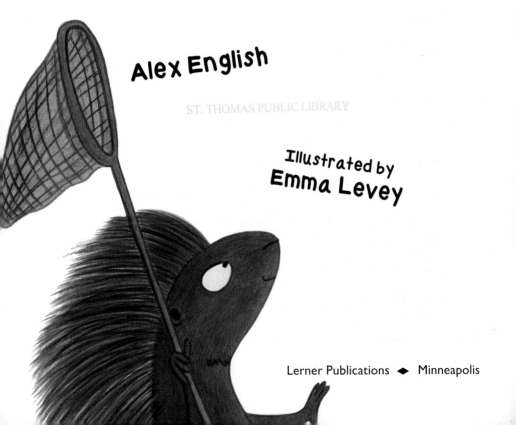

Lerner Publications ◆ Minneapolis

A porcupine went to see Sam.

"Good!" said Sam.

"You can play with me!"

"Shall we play with this?" said Sam.

"No, that is MINE!" said the porcupine.

"Shall we play with rockets?" said Sam.

"No, that rocket is mine!"

said the porcupine.

"There are lots of things
we can play!" said Sam.

"Or we can do a painting!" said Sam.

But the porcupine just said, "Mine!"

"MINE!"

"MINE!"

"MINE!"

Sam said, "All right. I will not play

with you. I will play in the land of Kaboo."

The land of Kaboo was fun.

Sam had fun jumping and running
and skidding.

He sang as he swung in the trees.

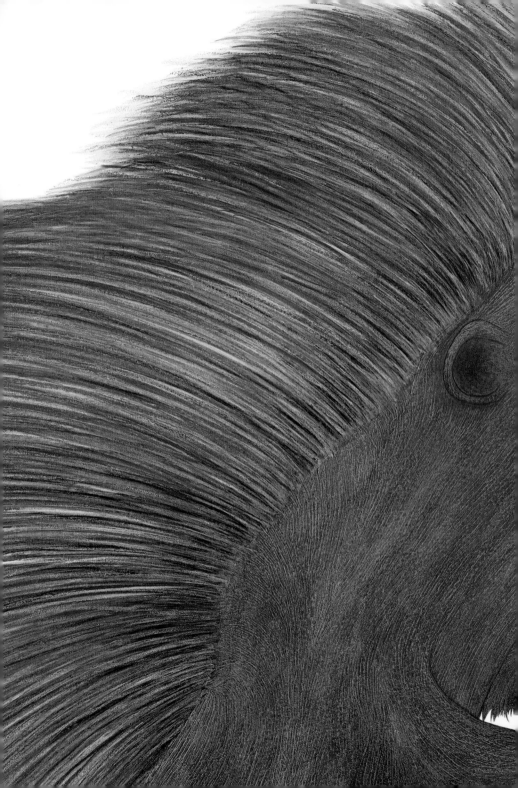

"Can I play too?" said the porcupine.

"Please?"

"Yes," said Sam. "Just grab my hand."

Sam and the porcupine ran off to play.

"Now you can be my best friend," said Sam.

"And you can be mine,"

said the porcupine.

Quiz

1. Who comes to Sam's house?
   a) A dog
   b) A porcupine
   c) A cat

2. What does the porcupine do?
   a) He takes Sam's toys.
   b) He runs away.
   c) He jumps on Sam's rocket.

3. But the porcupine just said . . . ?
   a) "Mine!"
   b) "Yuck!"
   c) "Bang!"

4. Sam goes to the land of . . . ?
   a) Rockets
   b) Porcupines
   c) Kaboo

5. Why can Sam and the porcupine play in the end?
   a) They sing together.
   b) Sam says "mine!"
   c) The porcupine says "please."

Leveled for Guided Reading

Early Bird Stories have been edited and leveled by leading educational consultants to correspond with guided reading levels. The levels are assigned by taking into account the content, language style, layout, and phonics used in each book.

COLOR		GRL
Blue		E-G
Yellow		C-E
Red		C-D
Pink		A-C

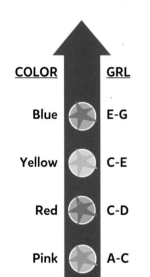